For Mum and Dad

Zzz...

MARGARET K. McELDERRY BOOKS

An imprint of Simon & Schuster Children's Publishing Division

1230 Avenue of the Americas, New York, New York 10020

Copyright © 2019 by Ellie Sandall

Originally published in Great Britain by Hodder Children's Books, a division of Hachette Children's Group

MARGARET K. McELDERRY BOOKS is a trademark of Simon & Schuster, Inc.

For information about special discounts for bulk purchases, please contact Simon & Schuster

Special Sales at 1-866-506-1949 or business@simonandschuster.com.

The Simon & Schuster Speakers Bureau can bring authors to your live event. For more information

or to book an event, contact the Simon & Schuster Speakers Bureau at 1-866-248-3049 or visit our website at

www.simonspeakers.com.

Book design by Ann Bobco

The text for this book was set in P22Garamouche.

Manufactured in China

1118 HCB

First Margaret K. McElderry Books edition February 2019

10 9 8 7 6 5 4 3 2 1

Library of Congress Cataloging-in-Publication Data

Names: Sandall, Ellie, author, illustrator.

Title: Everybunny dream! / Ellie Sandall.

Description: First edition. | New York : Margaret K. McElderry Books, [2019] | "Originally published in Great

Britain by Hodder Children's Books"—Copyright page. | Summary: After a busy day, young rabbits put on pajamas,

brush their teeth, trim their claws, snuggle into bed—and find a surprise.

Identifiers: LCCN 2018024747 (print) | LCCN 2018030519 (eBook)

| ISBN 9781534440043 (hardback) | ISBN 9781534440050 (eBook)

Subjects: | CYAC: Stories in rhyme. | Bedtime—Fiction. | Rabbits—Fiction. | BISAC: JUVENILE FICTION /

Animals / Rabbits. | JUVENILE FICTION / Bedtime & Dreams. | JUVENILE FICTION / Animals / General.

Classification: LCC PZ8.3.S217 (eBook) | LCC PZ8.3.S217 Evh 2019 (print) | DDC [E]—dc23

LC record available at https://lccn.loc.gov/2018024747

Ellie ☆ Sandall

EVERYBUNNY
Dream!

Zzz...

Zzz...

Margaret K. McElderry Books
New York • London • Toronto • Sydney • New Delhi

Little bunnies like to play.
They have had a busy day.

But now it's late and time to say . . .

EVERYBUNNY

Bedtime won't be very long.
Time to put pajamas on.

EVERYBUNNY WASH!

And brush your **teeth,**

and clean your **paws,**

and comb your **tail**,

and trim your **claws**.

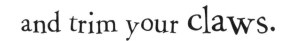

But **wait!**
Who's here
in the dark?
A quiet giggle,
muffled bark.

and say good night.

And cuddle up,
and snuggle tight,
and close your eyes,

Bunny ears
and bunny socks,

a bushy, orange tail . . .

A noise outside!
A sudden **knock.**
Some pointed ears . . .
another fox?

And huddle up,
and snuggle in.
A happy smile,
a cheeky grin.

A cozy group,
a peaceful scene.

Every fox cub,

everybunny . . .

dream.

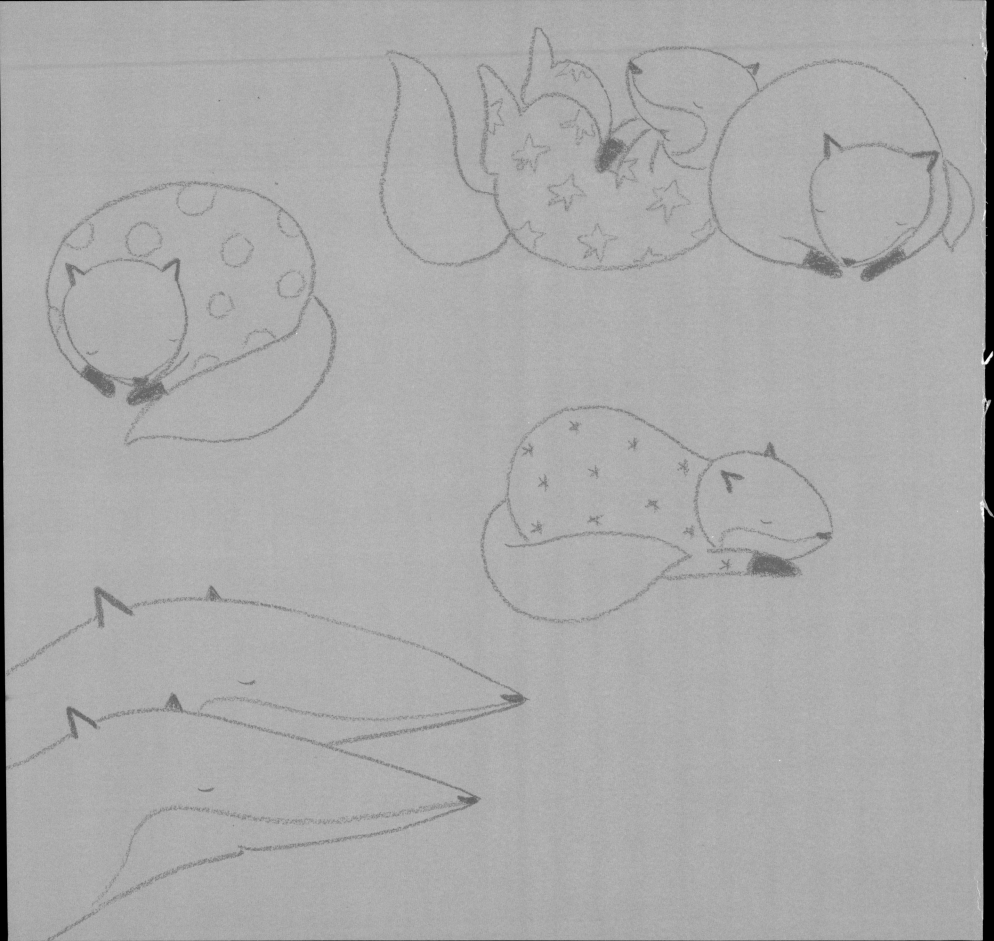